slow

passionate

soft

sweet

love

eager

desire

delicious

kisses galore

Your Daddy and me

First published by Pinter & Martin Ltd 2013

Text copyright © 2013 Mònica Calaf
Illustrations copyright © 2013 Mikel Fuentes

ISBN 978-1-78066-015-8

British Library Cataloguing-in-Publication Data
A catalogue record for this book is available from the British Library

Printed in the EU by Graficas 94, Spain

Pinter & Martin Ltd
6 Effra Parade
London SW2 1PS

www.pinterandmartin.com

Your Daddy and me

Text Mònica Calaf

Illustrations Mikel Fuentes
www.mifupa.com

pinter & martin

When I first started liking your Daddy
a whole new world of feelings
stirred inside me.

Whenever I saw him, it felt as if
my feet weren't touching the ground!
It was as if I were floating on a cloud of joy.

Whenever our eyes met,
I felt a wave of heat go through me
and my face turned bright red.

Whenever we got close to one another
and accidentally touched, my heart
began to race, and my tummy tingled
as if a thousand butterflies were
inside me.

He was so handsome, so interesting,
so different from all the other boys I knew...

He had stolen my heart!

I went out of my way to bump into
your Daddy! I was crazy about him...

The first time we met,
we talked and talked...

The next day, every time the phone rang, my heart skipped a beat!

We arranged to meet...

We made a great couple.
We went out to dinner...

We went to concerts...

We went to see shows...

We went to parties...

Shh!

Your Daddy and me

We went to the cinema...

We went on trips...
We went travelling...
We loved discovering new places!

We liked to dream about our plans
for the future and we told each other
our innermost secrets...

The love we felt for one another
grew stronger every day.

We always wanted to be together...

Your Daddy lived at home with his family
and I lived in another house with mine.

We wanted to be together all the time,
so we saved up enough money to
get a house of our own.

When we moved into our new house,
we threw a big party to celebrate.
It was a very special day!

We felt very happy because
now we could be together during
the day and at night...

Sometimes we quarrelled
over silly things...

...but we always made up in the end. We have had to get used to living together, and to learn how to respect and understand each other.

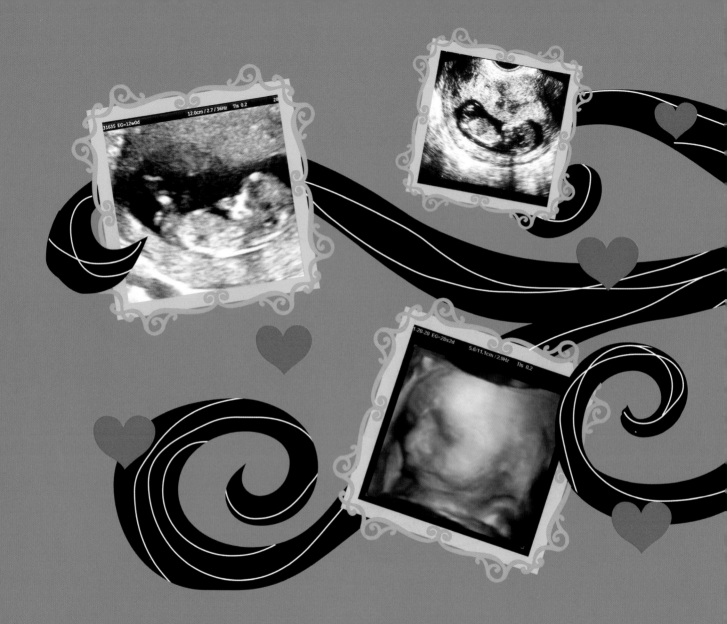

You were made out of our love, and you began to grow inside me. We were so happy that we were going to be parents!

That's the story of how your Daddy and I met,
and of how we decided to be together
and have a family of our own.

I hope you liked our story
Your Daddy and me!
Good night!

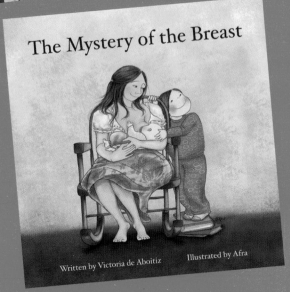